My Personal Panther

www.mypersonalpanther.com

"My Personal Panther"

is for my wife and hero, Pam.

And for my teacher, Doris Dixon.

And for millions of homeless cats and dogs suffering on streets and in alleys, abandoned and unloved. They are hungry, cold and frightened. Please visit a nearby shelter and give an abandoned animal a loving home.

ISBN 978-0-578-10507-9

Canyon Hawk Books

Most panthers are three
times bigger than she,
with long claws and coats dark and shiny.

But Aja's not tall,
and her claws are quite small.
I think she is beautifully tiny!

We start every day
in a panther-like way,
with a purr and a stretch and a yawn.

Then we brush teeth and hair,

and decide what to wear.

Then go downstairs, 'cause breakfast is on!

I think that most
people like jam and toast.
I have some each morning with cantelope.

But that's not a feast
for a fierce jungle beast.
So Mom will give Aja canned antelope.

As an every day rule
when I go off to school,
I tell Aja "You must behave!"

A busy day hunting and stalking.

Meanwhile back at home
where the wild creatures roam,
a small panther is on the loose.

Soon to jump on the back
of a fuzzy fat yak.
(who looks a lot like our dog, Zeus).

While perched up on high
as the yak wanders by,
Aja spies something dee-lish.

It's time to examine
some wild river salmon,
a panther's most favorite fish.

For lunch nothing beats a
slice of good pizza!
I like it with salad and juice.

And as you can tell,
Aja just loves gazelle.
She has it while lunching with Zeus.

And while she is sleeping,
I know she is keeping
me in her sweet panther dreams.

As an every day rule,
I really like school,
but I'm glad when it comes to an end.

It's been a long day
of being away
from my panther, my very best friend!

And then came the day,
a most horrible day,
when I got home and something was wrong.

A panther might hide
in a cave deep inside
where's it's quiet and perfect for sleeping.

Or up in a tree
where she's able to see
if a lizard or mongoose comes creeping.

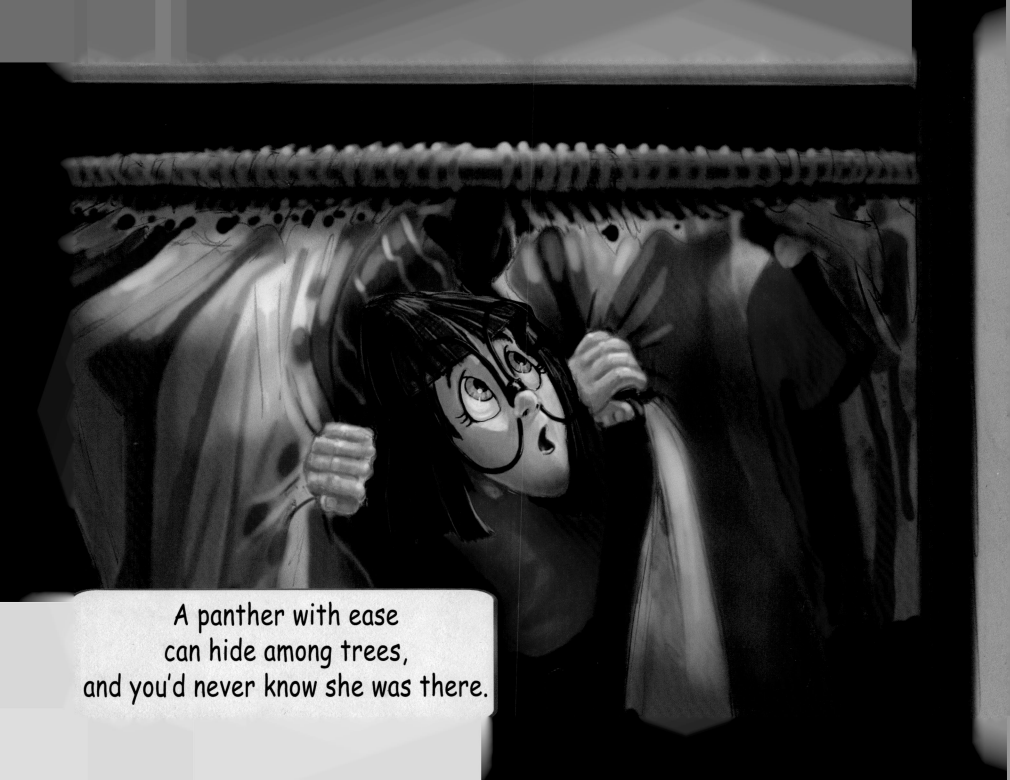

A panther with ease
can hide among trees,
and you'd never know she was there.

Mom helped me look
in each cranny and nook.
There wasn't a place that we spared.

Things had turned out quite right
on that once-scary night.
For my personal panther and me.

Thank you for reading our book!

And please thank the person
who bought it for you,
because
some of the money they spent
will protect animals.

Like cats and dogs.
And cows and pigs and chickens.
And certainly, panthers.

We'll see you in our next book!

We love you.

For Grown-ups

Next to Pam and the animals who share our home, the most important thing in my life is the
protection of animals. My great friend Wayne Pacelle, President and CEO of
The Humane Society of the United States wrote a marvelous book called "The Bond," in which he said,
"In our relationship with animals, we have all the power."
Which is why millions of animals suffer unspeakable cruelty on factory farms,
in laboratories, for "sport", fashion and entertainment.
Please join me in helping animals by joining The HSUS and AAVS.

www.hsus.org   www.aavs.org

And when your family wishes to share your home with a loving animal,
please adopt from your nearby animal shelter or rescue group.

That's where the "real" Aja came from.

All good wishes,

Visit Lucy & Aja at: www.mypersonalpanther.com